STOMPIN' AT THE SAVOY

For the dancing spirits that once filled the Savoy Ballroom—
may they Lindy Hop through eternity, and all the dancers yet to come. —B.M.C.

To Eric Carle, an artist whom I greatly admire, a special and beloved friend, and
a generous mentor. —R.Y.

BEBE MOORE CAMPBELL

Illustrated by RICHARD YARDE

STOMPIN' AT THE SAVOY

Philomel Books

As Mindy stared at her dinner, a big fat tear plopped right onto her collard greens. Her jazz dance recital would begin in less than four hours, and she was scared.

Her three great-aunties, Auntie Willa Mae, Auntie Naomi and Auntie Norma, were having a good time dancing, which is what they always did after dinner. Old-timey music blared from the CD player while the aunties practiced their steps. Dancing at home with them was okay. Dancing by herself was okay, but . . .

"I don't want to dance for strangers!" Mindy said in her whiny voice. "I might fall."

"Mercy," said Auntie Willa Mae and Auntie Norma, who held their ears.

"Stop whining," said Auntie Naomi. "It makes me climb the walls. All you have to do is move your happy feet, Li'l Bit. Whatever happens, just keep dancing."

Mindy shook her head. "If you make me dance in the recital," she shouted, "I'll run away."

She rushed into her room, slammed the door and flung herself across her bed. Tap. Tap. Mindy peeked out her window. Two drumsticks were beating a drum, and no one was around.

"I'm Patapataboomboomdaboomboom," the drum said. "I'm taking you to the
Home of Happy Feet."
A talking drum? "Somebody's trying to mess with my mind," Mindy said.

The drum started rolling with the sticks beating it. *Patapataboomboomdaboomboom.*
The next thing Mindy knew, she was snapping her fingers and following it
down the fire escape, way beneath the sidewalk to a place she'd never seen before.

There was a tall door with a sign in electric lights: the Savoy Ballroom. At the foot of the door was a black cat.

"Welcome," said the cat.

"Wow," Mindy said, stepping inside. The room was as huge as a playground, and the soft light above glowed like a new moon. On a long stage, a band was playing loud, joyful music. "A-tisket, a-tasket," sang a woman with a jazzy voice that made feet move. Dancers of all sizes and shapes were shaking and stomping, swinging and strutting!

But why were they wearing such out-of-style clothes and hairstyles? Mindy stared for a moment.

"Somebody's trying to mess with my mind," she said.

"Where are we, Patapata . . . ?" she asked.

But as she looked, the drum rolled onto the stage.

Listening to the music, Mindy felt as though someone had poured the rhythm inside her. Her head began bobbing. She began to snap her fingers as smiling dancers whirled and twirled around her. Sliding her feet back and forth as the

music grew louder and faster, Mindy swayed and clapped. And clapped. Then she stopped. Suppose people were watching her?

Suddenly there was a blare of trumpets, a ripple of loud piano chords and a crash of cymbals. The crowd began to cheer when two men appeared on the stage.

"Welcome, all you hepcats and satin dolls. My name is Chick Webb," said the first, waving drumsticks in the air.

"I'm Benny Goodman," said the second man, clutching a clarinet. "Let's quit jiving and get this battle started."

He put the instrument to his lips and blew. *Tweedledeedeedeedadadee.*
"Are they really going to fight?" Mindy asked a woman standing next to her.
The lady laughed. "Whoever has the best music wins." She looked closely at
Mindy. "There are no children allowed in the Savoy. And here comes the bouncer."

A huge man with fingers as big as sausages stood in front of her. Mindy danced right into the crowd. The bouncer was right behind her. She trucked among the legs and feet of the dancers and was soon bumped to the middle of the floor. The room seemed to be spinning around and around, with dancing feet everywhere.

Mindy couldn't stop dancing herself. She was gliding, and it felt as if her body was a drumbeat. *This really is the home of happy feet.* People stopped to watch her.

When she saw all the eyes on her, Mindy felt too shy to continue.

"Slip me some skin, little lady," a voice said.

Chick Webb stood in front of her, with his hand extended. Mindy slapped his hand with hers.

"Crazy! Come on up! I want you to be in the dance competition. The winner's prize is ten dollars."

Mindy whispered her name, and the next thing she knew, she was standing with about a dozen other people. They were practicing their steps as they waited their turn. Where was that bouncer now?

"Billy and Willa Mae!" the announcer shouted as Chick began drumming.

An energetic young couple took to the floor. Mindy had never seen their dance before! Someone behind her called it the Peabody. It looked like walking set to rhythm.

"Norma and George!"

A man and a woman who looked like teenagers held each other closely and danced slowly. Suddenly, they backed away from each other and started wiggling and shaking, as though they had ice cubes slipping down their backs. They clapped their hands as they twisted and did the shimmy. Then George pulled Norma close again and they ended the dance in slow motion.

No name for their dance.

"Frankie and Naomi!"

"The Lindy Hop," someone whispered.

Frankie and Naomi slid on their knees about ten feet to the stage, then jumped up, faced each other and began kicking their legs back and forth from side to side as Benny Goodman played. *Tweedledeedeedeedadadee.* Frankie put his arms around Naomi and spun her around so that her back was to him. Then he jumped over her head.

But as he was coming down, he lost his balance and toppled over. Mindy groaned, but Frankie bounced up, grinned at the audience and winked at Mindy.

"Mindy!"

Patapataboomboomdaboomboom. Mindy took a deep, deep breath and stepped onto the floor. *Whatever happens, I'll just keep dancing.* She arched her back and threw up her arms.

"Ladies and gentlemen, my jazz recital dance."

People formed a big circle around her and clapped.

Mindy was sure moving her happy feet!

She was about to leap into the air when she saw the bouncer.

"No children at the Savoy. Your time's up," he said, grabbing her wrist.

"Why don't you let the kid finish her dance," Frankie said to the bouncer.

"No children," the bouncer said, his voice a snarl.

The other dancers began chanting, "Let her dance!"

But the bouncer refused to let her go. How would she ever get back to her aunties? Mindy wished that she'd been sweet and pleasant to them before she left, instead of whining.

Maybe . . .

She looked at the bouncer. "Please," she said in her whiniest voice. "Pretty, pretty please."

"Don't start whining," said the bouncer, with a look of horror.

"Please, please, please let me go," Mindy whined. Frankie and Naomi put their fingers in their ears, as did the people closest to her.

"Hey, cut that out right now," the bouncer said, dropping her arm.

"Pleeeeeeeease," she cried.

Mindy's screechy baby voice was louder than Chick Webb's drums, higher than Benny Goodman's clarinet. So high that the people near her stopped dancing and covered their ears.

The bouncer backed away until he hit a wall. He turned and began to climb it! Up, up, up!

Horns blared from the bandstand. Frankie and Naomi grabbed Mindy and the three of them began Lindy Hopping across the floor. Just then, the bouncer jumped down from the wall and raced toward her. Frankie swung around, then grabbed Naomi's and Mindy's hands. He leaped and then flung his partners high into the air.

Mindy was so light that she sailed through a hole in the ceiling and past the black cat, who waved good-bye just as an announcer said, "And the winners of the battle of the bands and the dance contest are . . ."

Mindy landed with a thud on top of her own bed. *It doesn't matter who won.* When she looked up, her aunties were standing over her. The house was filled with old-timey music.

"Mindy, it's time for your recital," Auntie Willa Mae said, handing her the costume as she moved her head to the beat.

"I'm ready," Mindy said, "and I'm not afraid."

"Good girl," said Auntie Norma, hunching her shoulders up and down.

"Here's an ending for you, Li'l Bit," said Auntie Naomi. "Watch."

Patapataboomboomdaboomboom.

The aunties slid across the floor and did three perfect splits.

Mindy gave them a long, hard look. Could it be?
"Somebody is definitely trying to mess with my mind."

SAVOY HISTORICAL NOTE

Opened in Harlem, New York, in 1926, the Savoy Ballroom was home to the greatest dancers and musicians of the swing era. One of the few integrated ballrooms in America at the time, the Savoy featured jazz legends such as Ella Fitzgerald, Cab Calloway, Glenn Miller, and Count Basie, drawing visitors from around the world until its closing in 1958.

I would like to acknowledge the support and help of: Susan Yarde, Bebe Moore Campbell, my sons Marcus and Owen-Donovan, my grandson Jared, Pat Gauch, Semadar Megged, Larry Schulz, Katrina and Katherine Fulmer, Chris Peters of Paradise Copies, Melvin and Dallas Jackson, Claudio Guerra, Joseph Plaskett, and Terry Monaghan.   —R.Y.

Patricia Lee Gauch, Editor

PHILOMEL BOOKS

A division of Penguin Young Readers Group.   Published by The Penguin Group.
Penguin Group (USA) Inc., 375 Hudson Street, New York, NY 10014, U.S.A.
Penguin Group (Canada), 90 Eglinton Avenue East, Suite 700, Toronto, Ontario, Canada M4P 2Y3 (a division of Pearson Penguin Canada Inc.)
Penguin Books Ltd, 80 Strand, London WC2R 0RL, England.
Penguin Ireland, 25 St. Stephen's Green, Dublin 2, Ireland (a division of Penguin Books Ltd.)
Penguin Group (Australia), 250 Camberwell Road, Camberwell, Victoria 3124, Australia (a division of Pearson Australia Group Pty Ltd).
Penguin Books India Pvt Ltd, 11 Community Centre, Panchsheel Park, New Delhi - 110 017, India.
Penguin Group (NZ), Cnr Airborne and Rosedale Roads, Albany, Auckland 1310, New Zealand (a division of Pearson New Zealand Ltd).
Penguin Books (South Africa) (Pty) Ltd, 24 Sturdee Avenue, Rosebank, Johannesburg 2196, South Africa.
Penguin Books Ltd, Registered Offices: 80 Strand, London WC2R 0RL, England.

Text copyright © 2006 by Bebe Moore Campbell.   Illustration copyright © 2006 by Richard Yarde.

Design by Semadar Megged.   The illustrations are rendered in gouache and pastel on paper.

Library of Congress Cataloging-in-Publication Data
Campbell, Bebe Moore, 1950–   Stompin' at the Savoy / Bebe Moore Campbell ; [illustrations by] Richard Yarde.   p. cm.
Summary: On the night of her jazz dance recital Mindy feels too nervous to go, until a magical drum whisks her away to the Savoy Ballroom in Harlem where she finds her "happy feet." [1. Jazz dance—Fiction. 2. Dance recitals—Fiction. 3. Dance—Fiction. 4. African Americans—Fiction. 5. Harlem (New York, N.Y.)—History—20th century—Fiction.] I. Yarde, Richard, 1939– ill. II. Title.   PZ7.C15079Sto 2006   [Fic]—dc22   2005025044
ISBN 0-399-24197-3   10 9 8 7 6 5 4 3 2 1
First Impression